The Witch's Path

JJ Page

Illustrated by Penny Nicoles

FriesenPress

One Printers Way
Altona, MB R0G 0B0
Canada

www.friesenpress.com

Illustrator: Penny Nicoles

ISBN
978-1-03-830264-9 (Hardcover)
978-1-03-830263-2 (Paperback)
978-1-03-830265-6 (eBook)

1. JUVENILE FICTION, FANTASY & MAGIC

Distributed to the trade by The Ingram Book Company

The Witch's Path

Dedicated to kith and kindred.
For all who helped inspire me.

There was a witch, who lived in a mushroom house
Where all were welcome, even the field mouse.
Behind the house lay a forest so dense,
One could easily get lost and stop making sense.

The witch knew the woods like the back of her hand,

But not everyone had a knowledge so grand.

One day in the forest, the witch heard a strange sound

So she followed the noise and looked all around.

Under a thorn bush, she found a frightened young boy
Crying and scared, like he had lost all joy.
As she helped him stand, she asked, "Why are you alone?"
He said, "I heard music, so I followed it on my own."

It became quite clear what had happened to the boy.

He had been the victim of a mean fairy ploy.

Luckily, the witch knew just what to do.

She called out to the forest, her voice clear and true.

"Spirits of these woods, you know me well.

We would like to leave this place where you dwell.

We mean no offense, my fun loving friends,

So show us the way through the twists and bends.

I promise to return with energy anew.

I'll come tomorrow, when the sky is bright and blue."

Then the trees seemed to move and a path suddenly cleared.
The witch took the boy's hand and down the trail she steered.
As she walked him to safety through the dense wood,
She told him of the fairies and to avoid them if he could.

"The forest is a natural and beautiful place.
It deserves our respect, and to be treated with grace.
The trees are home to owls and the caves home to bats.
The woods give them safety that the big city lacks.

That twisted old stump may look like it is dead,
But it's a home where the pixies lay their head.

Medicine can be made from many of these plants.
There is much to learn if you get a chance.
Dandelion can help relieve the pain of gout
And snakeroot will cure a cough, without a doubt.

Skullcap is calming for when there is stress.
But in the forest, don't dare make a mess.
Many beings make this place their home.
Be sure you're respectful wherever you roam.

Fairies can be sly and tricky, you know.
If you near a fairy ring, be careful as you go.
One misstep can lead you astray, to a different place.
Where fairies rule, and humans vanish without a trace."

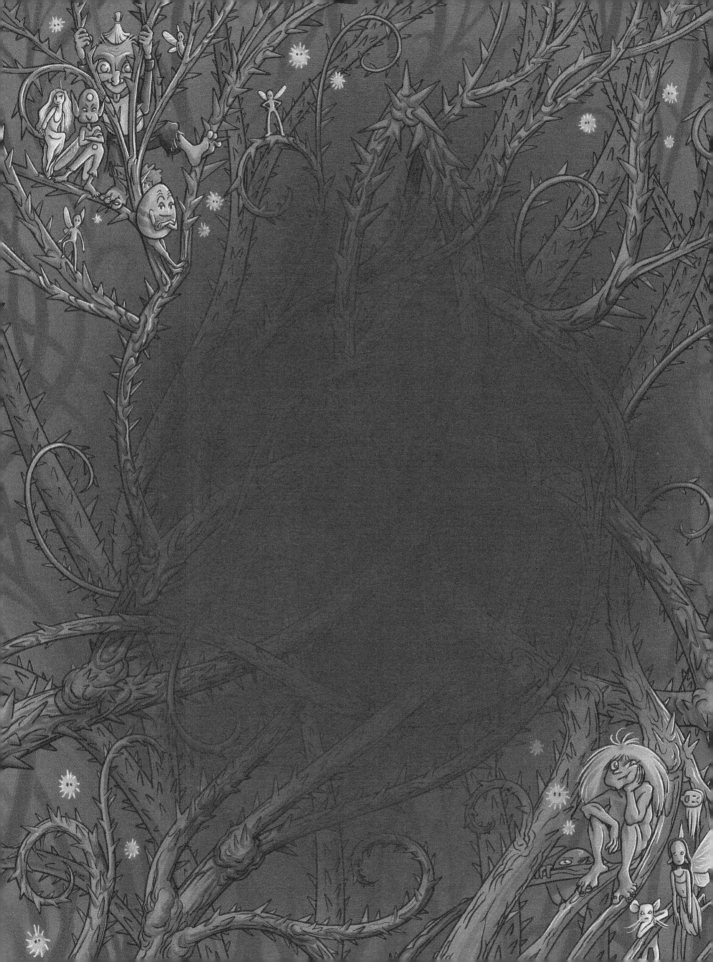

They walked until they reached the edge of the wood

Where a solid wall of thorny brambles stood.

It seemed the forest spirits were not satisfied.

The boy was afraid, but the witch took it in stride.

She took from her basket, a bottle of mead

Milk, honey, and a handful of birdseed.

She mixed the ingredients in a white bowl,

Then told the boy, "We must pay a small toll."

She had him pour the mixture onto the ground.
Then they waited for their offering to be found.
It didn't take long before the brambles moved aside

So they were free of the woods, the boy and his guide.

"A gift for a gift." The kind witch told the boy.

"We must give back when we take, so all can enjoy."

With this lesson taught, the witch saw the boy home,

Greeting his parents, so he would not be alone.

So happy were they to have their boy found,

They hugged him so tight that his feet left the ground.

The witch then went home, happy with her day.

She was glad she found the boy who was led astray.

There are many lessons from the forest to learn,

It's a wondrous place, but you must show some concern.

Don't break branches, or trample toadstools.

You'll be safe and sound if you follow these rules.

Don't follow strange laughter or stray from the path.

Don't start any fires or you'll incur the fairies' wrath.

We can all live in harmony with every forest,

Just be wary when you hear a fairy chorus.

Printed in the USA
CPSIA information can be obtained
at www.ICGtesting.com
JSHW061443081024
71134JS00008B/84